Bob's Cab

by Sue Graves and Michael Emmerson

Bob got into the cab.

"We can go now,"
said Bob.

3

Kim and her duck
got into the cab.

"We can go now,"
said Bob.

Bess and her chick
got into the cab.

"We can go now,"
said Bob.

6

Pam and her rabbit
got into the cab.

"We can go now,"
said Bob.

Jan and her cat
got into the cab.

"We can go now,"
said Bob.

Lin and her dog
got into the cab.

"We can go now,"
said Bob.

Deb and her goat
got into the cab.

"We can go now,"
said Bob.

"We can not go now,"
said Bob.

Everyone got into the bus.

"We can go now,"
said Bob.

Story trail

Start at the beginning of the story trail. Ask your child to retell the story in their own words, pointing to each picture in turn to recall the sequence of events.

Start

Independent Reading

This series is designed to provide an opportunity for your child to read on their own. These notes are written for you to help your child choose a book and to read it independently.

In school, your child's teacher will often be using reading books which have been banded to support the process of learning to read. Use the book band colour your child is reading in school to help you make a good choice. *Bob's Cab* is a good choice for children to read independently who are reading at Red Band in their classroom.

The aim of independent reading is to read this book with ease, so that your child enjoys the story and relates it to their own experiences.

About the book

In this story, Bob's cab is tested when lots of passengers and their pets get on. Soon the cab is too full and breaks down!

Before reading

Help your child to learn how to make good choices by asking:
"Why did you choose this book? Why do you think you will enjoy it?"
Support your child to think about what they already know about the story context. Look at the cover together and ask: "What do you think the story will be about?" Read the title aloud and ask:
"What are the people and their pets doing?"
Remind your child that they can try to sound out the letters to make a word if they get stuck.
Decide together whether your child will read the story independently or read it aloud to you. When books are short, as at Red Band, your child may wish to do both!

During reading

If reading aloud, support your child if they hesitate or ask for help by telling the word. Remind your child of what they know and what they can do independently.

If reading to themselves, remind your child that they can come and ask for your help if stuck.

After reading

Support comprehension by asking your child to tell you about the story. Help your child think about the messages in the book that go beyond the story and ask: "Why did everyone get on a bus at the end of the story?"

Give your child a chance to respond to the story: "Did you have a favourite part? Would you like to ride in a cab like this? Why/Why not"

Use the story trail to encourage your child to retell the story in the right sequence, in their own words.

Extending learning

Help your child extend the story structure by using the same sentence pattern and adding some more elements. For example, Bev and her rat got into the cab. Nic and her mouse got into the cab.

On a few of the pages, check your child can finger point accurately by asking them to show you how they kept their place in the print by tracking from word to word.

Help your child to use letter information by asking them to find the interest word on each page by using the first letter. For example: "Which word is 'rabbit'? How did you know it was that word?"

Franklin Watts
First published in Great Britain in 2017
by The Watts Publishing Group

Series Editors: Jackie Hamley and Melanie Palmer
Series Advisors: Dr Sue Bodman and Glen Franklin
Series Designer: Peter Scoulding

A CIP catalogue record for this book is
available from the British Library.

ISBN 978 1 4451 5353 7 (hbk)
ISBN 978 1 4451 5354 4 (pbk)

Printed in China

Franklin Watts
An imprint of
Hachette Children's Group
Part of The Watts Publishing Group
Carmelite House
50 Victoria Embankment
London EC4Y 0DZ

An Hachette UK Company
www.hachette.co.uk

www.franklinwatts.co.uk

FSC
www.fsc.org
MIX
Paper from
responsible sources
FSC® C104740